Dynamo Island

The Cultural History and Geography of a Utopia

T0154596

Dynamo Island

The Cultural History and Geography of a Utopia

David Scott

Winchester, UK
Washington, USA

First published by Zero Books, 2016
Zero Books is an imprint of John Hunt Publishing Ltd., Laurel House, Station Approach,
Alresford, Hants, SO24 9JH, UK
office1@jhpbooks.net
www.johnhuntpublishing.com
www.zero-books.net

For distributor details and how to order please visit the 'Ordering' section on our website.

Text copyright: David Scott 2015

ISBN: 978 1 78535 112 9
Library of Congress Control Number: 2015937452

A CIP catalogue record for this book is available from the British Library.

Design: Stuart Davies

Printed and bound by CPI Group (UK) Ltd, Croydon, CR0 4YY, UK

We operate a distinctive and ethical publishing philosophy in all
areas of our business, from our global network of authors to
production and worldwide distribution.

CONTENTS

List of Illustrations

1. Dynamo national flag
2. Map of Dynamo
3. St David's Cathedral, Veloxeter
4. Relief map of Dynamo
5. *Arcadian Landscape* by Alfred Sizzler
6. Dynamo Island badge
7. *Velox Waterways* by William Schooner
8. Roman Amphitheatre, Boxcaster
9. *Olympia Countryside* by Paul Mash
10. View of Odessa
11. Aero Dynamo airline logo
12. Government Buildings, Veloxeter (architect: Henry Scott)
13. *Back of Old Mills, Hubcaster, men wading* by John Chrome
14. *Headwaters of the River Crease* by John Spell
15. *Campana Farmhouse* by Ivan Lichen
16. *View of Anasi* by Henry Woodcock
17. *Metal Workshops, Rugby* by Fortunato Desperado
18. Dynamo Rails, Dynamo Trams – company logos
19. *Handlebar Mountains from the East* by Alfred Sizzler
20. View of Oarhouse, Spokane
21. *Maurice Island* by William Schooner
22. *Entry to Quinnport* by Eric Ravisher
23. Dynamo Island stamps
24. *Mount Eoin, Pugilia* by Henry Woodcock
25. National sports-club badges

For Taian, Finn and Loic

'the concrete dictatorship of the automobile, which has swallowed an entire civilization'
(Jean Baudrillard, *Technics as Social Practice*, 1968)

1. Dynamo National Flag

Acknowledgements

I am very grateful to my friend and colleague Robin Fuller for his encouragement, guidance and practical assistance in preparing this project. I also wish to thank to Kevin Breathnach for his critical feedback and advice on editorial matters. The work on the project was facilitated and made enjoyable by two separate weeks in 2013 and 2014 working in Ballinskelligs, Co. Kerry, Ireland, under the generous auspices of The Cill Rialaig Project.

Introduction

Dynamo Island, situated in the North Atlantic Ocean on a similar latitude to France, is about the size of England. Roughly circular in shape, it has high granitic (Cambrian) mountains along its western extremity (the Handlebar Mountains) with long limestone escarpments (the Freewheel Plains) stretching eastward. As the prevailing winds are westerly, the rainfall in the mountains is high, resulting in dense deciduous forest with many rushing streams. The island's main river, the Crease, gathers many eastward lowing tributaries before reaching its mouth in a long estuary at Veloxeter, the country's capital and main port.

Lacking significant reserves of coal or oil, the country's government from the beginning of the twentieth century developed a policy of maximal energy conservation and intense environmental protection. Over half of the country's electricity is generated by waterpower, with about a third by tide and wind power. A highly developed public transport system based on electric trains and trams obviated the necessity for cars. On short trips, city- and country-dwellers alike use bikes, with many in the country travelling by pony and trap. Since there are no tractors, carthorses continue to do the work of ploughing and haulage. This has resulted in a slower rhythm of work but one that has no negative environmental impact. An intensive recycling system means that little is wasted and there is a national ban on plastic (except for electronic, medical and communicational goods). Pesticides and all artificial fertilisers are also banned. All fowl and animals are free-range, the concept of factory-farming being unknown.

This approach to agriculture and the environment means that

the country's internal economy is as much based on local self-sufficiency and regional exchange as on the centralised, supermarket culture of Europe and North America. Every house in the country is encouraged to have its own garden and every small town has its weekly market. Although predominantly agrarian, the country is quite rich since its cheap and abundant electrical power has enabled it to develop sophisticated electrical and mechanical technology. It is a world leader in bicycle design. Though lacking in coal and oil, the country has good reserves of iron ore and, in the Handlebar Mountains, base metals.

A national computer and telecommunications network promotes work at home and reduces the need for daily travel. As a further saving in power, the country's towns and cities use their street-lights only between sundown and 1am, while in the country – owing to the lack of pollution and light interference – people are less dependent on artificial light. All bikes and pony traps are fitted with dynamos and all homes powered by solar panels. Wood fires are permitted but only if fuelled by faggots collected in the country's many oak and beech forests.

Dynamo is a democratic Republic, without monarchy or aristocracy, with a population of 20 million people. There is no national religion, though faiths are tolerated provided they do not assert their differences in ostentatious communitarianism. An ancient mythology attached to agrarian, maritime and sporting accomplishments is popularly cultivated and reflected in many regional team mascots and badges. The national flag is a rectangle divided longwise, with the upper band (blue) representing the sky, the lower (green) the earth. In the centre figures a white wheel with eight spokes, the symbolic dynamo linking earth and sky and ensuring a cyclical replenishment of both spheres. The circle is a national symbol, promoted both as an aesthetic principle and as a model of community and of energy, mobility and productivity.

Self-deprecatory humour is a national characteristic and although individual success is admired and encouraged, much importance is attached to teamwork and communal effort. The western cult of celebrity is looked on with scepticism. Pleasure and self-fulfilment are encouraged in particular through outdoor activities, sports, games and entertainment. The country produces fine wines and beers, excellent fish, fruit and vegetables. All drugs and stimulants (including alcohol) are legalised, though those imported from abroad are expensive, and addiction is strongly discouraged. The island is conscious of its status as a cog in the larger global wheel but fully aware of its function and of the need to produce energy in a way that is not harmful to its environment, national or international.

It is not by accident that cycling is the country's national sport. It is promoted not only as an enjoyable sport in its own right, as an excellent form of exercise for both sexes and all ages, and as a highly efficient means of transport, but also for *ethical* reasons: the bicycle enables humans to enter into a constructive relationship with the physical environment in which energy, movement and a sense of the real resistance and forces at play in the natural world and in the human body are recognised. The idea of producing power from human energy that is put to human use within a balanced ecological equation is central to Dynamo Island's understanding of man's role in the world. The dynamo principle thus became central to the island community's ethos and is reflected not only in the country's name but also in much of its national symbolism. The annual Tour of Dynamo cycle race, which lasts for ten days and is open to men and women within a wide range of categories, constitutes a kind of national celebration of this principle. In taking its participants on a spectacular route through all the eight provinces of the country it also draws public attention to the beauty and variety of the island's natural scenery.

The aim of the following cultural history and geography of Dynamo is to explore ways in which it would be possible for a European culture based in a temperate latitude to live in harmonious relationship with its environment while fully exploring human potential in terms of physical, mental and moral development. The account aims to show that the elimination of just one major but pernicious environmental factor – that of the internal combustion engine – could transform human (and animal) life and make possible in the modern world an interaction with nature as harmonious as that of the remaining indigenous tribes scattered across the remoter parts of the globe. By checking the infinitely experimental propensities of *Homo faber* and in the process establishing a communally agreed equation by which 'progress' is always balanced by the acquired wisdom of the past, Dynamoans, it is argued, have created a society that is in close communication and interaction with the physical and elemental reality of the phenomenal world while still enjoying the infinite scope for creativity opened up by human interactions within a tolerant and imaginative society. Such a project would of course depend on a heightened awareness of the role of history in human affairs and the need for a combined sense of individual and communal identity and responsibility in the face of the phenomenal world.

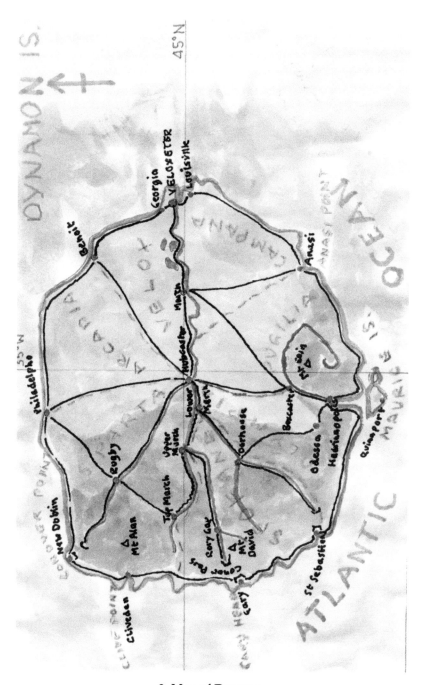

2. Map of Dynamo

Chapter 1

Arriving in Veloxeter

The best way to arrive in Dynamo, as in any island, however large, is by boat, especially since the country's capital city, Veloxeter, is a port that opens generous arms to vessels arriving in from the Eastern Atlantic. The perfume of the island with its luscious vegetation and clean air mixes energisingly with the salt of the ocean, and the expectant traveller's excitement at arrival is heightened as the boat approaches the port in which fishing vessels and other coastal craft (berthed on the north side), merchant ships (moored to the south) and liners (docking on the city water-front to the west) manoeuvre in a colourful regatta, joined by yachts and pleasure craft from the marina.

3: St David's Cathedral, Veloxeter

The city's low but expansive architectural profile is dominated by the dome of St David's Cathedral, which sits like a grandiose soup-tureen cover over the surrounding buildings. The warehouses and depots, in various shades of grime-free red brick, that line the cobbled wharves, emit a range of exotic smells according to the merchandises they contain, so that whiffs of coffee and tea intermingle with timber and tar and the fragrance emitted by the avenues of limes that lead from the quay-side to the city centre.

One of the first things one notices is the absence of cars and lorries, which are unknown in Dynamo. Containers and heavy merchandise are unloaded from ships by crane onto electrically powered lighters that deliver them to one or other of the two railway termini situated to the north and south of the harbour. Or to smaller craft that will ship commodities upriver to inland destinations. The River Crease, which enters the sea through Veloxeter harbour, is navigable inland as far as Hubcaster, 250k upstream.

The passenger ship terminal is in the centre of the waterfront: a white art-deco building resembling the bridge and forecastle of a liner, it ushers new arrivals through customs and passport control and then disgorges them into a tree-lined square where trams are waiting to take them to any number of destinations within the city, as well as to the railways stations. And there are hundreds of pedal-powered rickshaws that will deliver individuals to any specific address within a radius of a few kilometres: their bronzed and strong-limbed riders are renowned for their cheerfulness and stamina, and the light bike-drawn carriages are painted in a rainbow spectrum of colours.

Though dating back to the late Roman era, Veloxeter developed and expanded in the medieval period, superseding Hubcaster as capital of the country in the seventeenth century. Its cathedral, popularly known as the 'soup tureen', is a baroque building with a large but shallow copper dome, situated a few hundred metres upstream from the river mouth. Built of limestone quarried in Sparta, it shares with the National Library and the university, both founded in the eighteenth century, the same honey-coloured hue. The naval defences situated to the north of the harbour are built of local chalk, set off by the grey-blue slates, mined in the Handlebar Mountains. The railways stations, one north and one to the south of the city centre, are built in light-coloured brick, similar to that of the National College of Design that also dates from the nineteenth century. The brickwork of these buildings, in a Venetian Byzantine style, is enlivened by decorative tiles and other glazed motifs that enhance their festive appearance.

Most of the city's major monuments of the twentieth century – the National Athletics, Boxing, Football and Rugby stadiums, the Architectural Institute, the Passenger terminal and the main cinemas and shopping streets – are art deco, making the city one of the richest examples of this style in the world. A distinctive feature of the sports stadiums and Art College is the way their façades are decorated with stylised reliefs of the activities they house, reflecting a general aim in Dynamo whereby the fronts of buildings act as an index to their functions. The Botanic Gardens, which double as a city-centre park, are laid out round beautiful cast-iron glass-houses produced by the same British and Irish foundries that produced buildings for Kew and Glasnevin.

A feature of the city is the way leisure and sporting amenities are spread out within a one- or two-kilometre radius of the centre, thus enhancing their accessibility and ensuring many green spaces within the built-up parts of the town. The absence of cars means there are no car parks and the streets and avenues of the city are unencumbered with vehicles, except for the small electric taxis and the thousands of pedal-powered rickshaws. Street noise is reduced to a constant light whirring interspersed with bicycle bells and taxi hooters. The River Crease is a busy thoroughfare with water taxis and ferries as well as passenger and cargo ships plying up and downstream to and from Hubcaster. So the sound of ships' horns and ferry bells adds distinctively to the urban hubbub.

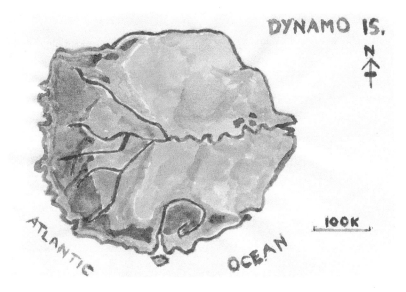

4: Relief Map of Dynamo

Chapter 2

Geology and Geography

Situated in the mid-Atlantic Ocean (35 degrees West) at a latitude similar to that of France (45 degrees North), Dynamo is an island of approximately 150,000 square kilometres. Roughly circular in shape (it is 450km wide and 400km long), the island seems to swim like a green Angel Fish in the blue waters of the Atlantic. Alternatively, with the multiple tributaries of the main river, the Crease, flowing eastwards from the Handlebar Mountains to deliver their waters to the sea at the deep estuary at Veloxeter, the island appears like a placenta floating in the ocean. Unaffected by the glaciations that sculpted the landscapes of northern Europe and America, the island has a fairly regular physical geography. Granitic mountains rise up to 2000 metres in the west and provide the watershed for the River Crease and its four main tributaries (from north to south: Pitch, Wicket, Oar and Rafter). The Crease rises at the mountains' highest peak, Mount David (2000m), while its northerly tributary, the Pitch, flows down from Mount Alan (1500m). The headwaters of the Crease cut back through the Handlebar Mountains at the Rory Gap from whence the Connor Pass provides a high route through the westerly heights before descending steeply to Port Gary on the island's west coast. A southern spur of the Handlebar Mountains continues eastwards along the southern coast of the island for some 250km, terminating in the Ring Mountains, whose highest peak is Mount Eoin (1000m). The eastern spur is divided by the River Antinous which, rising in the Ring Mountains, flows in an almost complete circle from Mt Eoin eastwards, then northwards, then westwards to Boxcaster, whence it flows south to join the sea in a spectacular bay at Hadrianopolis, opposite the green gem that is Maurice Island.

Approximately 100km from the steep and rocky west coast, the Handlebar Mountains descend to then disappear beneath the broad limestone planes (up to 500m high) that slope eastwards to create the vast fertile lowlands of Arcadia, Velox and Campana. The rich alluvium carried by the Crease and its tributaries slows the main river considerably the nearer it reaches its estuary, with many meanders and lakes along the last 150km of the river's course. Towards the eastern side of the country, the limestone strata in turn disappear beneath chalk that ends abruptly in the white cliffs that characterise the island's eastern seaboard. Precipitation in the lofty mountain of the west coast is high (up to 80 cm in some areas) but falls off to around 60 cm in the east, with figures as low as 50 cm in the northeast.

Though lacking in coal and oil, the fast-flowing rivers gushing down from the Handlebar Mountains provide massive hydro-electric power. This power, along with the presence of deposits of iron ore (Sparta), tin, copper and lead (Sparta), silver, gold and lead (Spokane) has led to the establishment of important metal-lurgical industries, with iron and steel at Rugby (Sparta). The main cities along the Wicket and the Crease (Top March, Upper March and Lower March) are noted for their sophisticated engineering and electronic industries, including computer, camera and media technology. Lower March, at the confluence of the Crease and the Rafter, is famous for its Institute of Technology (DIT). Oarhouse, at the confluence of the Oar and Rafter, is the centre of the country's paper-milling and recycling industries using the carefully managed resources of the richly timbered Handlebar Mountains. Oarhouse is also famous for its boat-building industries and for its electric locomotive and carriage workshops.

At the confluence of the Pitch and the Crease, Hubcaster, as its name suggests, is at the centre of the island's river and rail networks. It is the country's most important milling and agricultural processing centre (sugar, wheat, barley, potatoes, leguminous crops) and a leader in agricultural engineering. It is also the country's chief brewing centre (beer, cider, stout, whiskey), famous throughout the world for its Henry Tudor lager. The capital city, Veloxeter, at the mouth of the River Crease, is the country's business and financial centre, the home of marine, aeronautical and bicycle engineering and centre for the manufacture of leather goods, sports gear and clothing.

The fertile lowlands of East Sparta, Velox, Campana, Pugilia and Olympia produce the country's food requirements. In addition to sugar, wheat, barley, potatoes and legumes, the southern provinces are noted for their orchards and soft fruit farms, with vines being cultivated on the southern slopes of the Curran and Ring Mountains in Olympia and Pugilia respectively. Anasi and Benoit are both important brewing centres while Philadelpho is the centre of the island's wool industry. West Campana and Velox are the main dairying and market gardening regions. The country's main fishing ports are situated on the north and west coasts: Saint Sebastian, Port Gary, Cliveden, New Dublin and Philadelpho.

5: *Arcadian Landscape* **by Alfred Sizzler**

Chapter 3

The Woods of Arcadia

A particularity of Arcadia is that it seems more or less uninhabited. The north-eastern coast between Benoit and Philadelpho harbours only a few fishing ports while the vast hinterland is dotted with only a few regional towns, the exception being the major regional capital, Hubcaster. This is because, for some reason, the province, in its historic past, was subject to relatively little forest clearance, half of it remaining to this day covered in deciduous forests – oak, beech, ash and elm. To further the sense of wild naturalness, Arcadians tend to build their cottages low and to hide them behind thick hedges or banks, with the result that trotting in a pony-trap down some of the remoter country lanes, the only evidence of habitation is the greyish whorl and mellow odour of peat or wood smoke curling above a thicket of honeysuckle or eglantine. The farms are small and such clearings and meadows as exist among the woods are irregular in shape, not unlike the *bocage* scenery typical of western Normandy in France. Also as in Normandy, the farm buildings and cottages are built of timber and white- or pink-painted plaster, a style that is retained even on the most recently constructed buildings, the vernacular style being preserved, in its local variations, consistently throughout the country. Pigs, hens, geese, ducks and goats are allowed to range more or less free within the farm enclosure so the region is famous for the flavour and tenderness of its meat. It is also famed for the game that is plentiful in its woods and in the wilder moors that stretch across the north-western part of the county. Here many sheep are reared on the purple heaths and have made Philadelpho an important wool-processing centre.

Arcadia is a favourite place for the hunting, shooting and fishing that are still widely practised throughout Dynamo, although there are strict controls on the use of fire-arms and the quotas of game or animals that can be killed. The province is also rich in pasture and noted for its cheeses and milk products, as also for its paté de foie gras. The local towns, dreading to appear too urban, tend to straggle along one or two lengthy streets, much interspersed with ponds, thickets or other pockets of countryside. The streets themselves are seldom fully built-up, consisting rather of clumps of houses or buildings, the inns, workshops, retail stores and bicycle repair shops (standard throughout Dynamo, even in the smallest towns) remaining proudly detached from each other. Since there are no cars in Dynamo, the need for horses and ponies, and thus blacksmiths, saddlers and cart-wrights, means that much of the inner part of the province appears today much as it would have done in the eighteenth century. Only the telegraph poles that follow the lanes (which insist, often idiosyncratically, on the direction of the villages they connect), cycle-paths and the electric train or tramlines that cast a thin web across the province, attest to modernity.

6: Dynamo Island badge

Chapter 4

Flora and Fauna

As Dynamo Island did not experience glaciation in either of the two most recent Ice Ages, the native flora escaped the eradication of many species that occurred in the Northern British Isles. Dynamo therefore has a flora as rich and varied as that of France. Since the beginning of the twentieth century, when the government of the country adopted a rigorous policy of environmental protection very few of Dynamo's native species – plant, animal, bird, fish or insect – have died out. General public awareness of the importance of the natural world – from a scientific, aesthetic and cultural point of view – means that the country's wide range of species are popularly appreciated and protected. Each of the state's eight provinces uses a native plant as its emblem: Arcadia: Laurel; Campana: Oak; Maurice Island: Thrift or Sea Pink; Olympia: Ash; Pugilia: Boxglove; Sparta: Rugby Pine; Spokane: Periwinkle; Velox: Willow; each of these natural symbols is in turn associated with each province's favourite sport – Riding, Soccer, Sailing, Rowing, Boxing, Rugby, Cycling and Cricket respectively. These emblems are combined into a circular motif to constitute the national badge or logo.

The Romans introduced many Mediterranean plants into Dynamo in the same way that they did to Britain, and there is a fine herbarium of native plants at the Botanic Gardens in Veloxeter. The state's strict environmental laws mean however that unwanted exotics – spreading from ports and railway stations – that have in the later twentieth century blighted many sites in Europe, are systematically uprooted so that Buddleja, Canadian Golden Rod, Fuchsia, Russian Vine, Rhododendron and other plants are rarely to be seen outside private gardens. Although certain species of wild orchid and other rare plants are protected, in practice the native respect for all wild plants is in most cases protection enough. The prohibition of the use of artificial fertilisers and insecticides means that the cornfields of Camapana and Pugilia are in the summer ablaze with poppies, corn cockle and cornflower, while the meadows of Velox and Sparta are rich in wildflowers. Similarly, the high standard of purity of all the island's waterways means that they are rich in native plant, animal and insect life. Chance invasions of exotic species of plant or waterweed are ruthlessly rooted out.

Birds, animals and insects are similarly protected as vital parts of the ecological cycle. The Purple Emperor butterfly is therefore a common sight in the beech woods of Arcadia while the Swallowtail butterfly is locally plentiful in the fenlands of Velox. The island's many seasonal visitors and long coast in the mid-Atlantic mean that there are many seabirds, including Albatrosses and Terns. The wild animals of Dynamo are of similar species to those found in Western Europe, with wild boar still roaming some of the remoter forests, and bears in the high mountains. Dynamo Island's position in the rich Atlantic fisheries means that plentiful supplies of most species are available, though once again stocks are protected by a rigorous government quota policy. Shellfish are particularly plentiful along the island's rocky western coast. The cleanliness of the rivers and island waterways means that angling is a sport that is enjoyed profitably in most parts of the country. Shooting and hunting are also widespread but carefully controlled sports.

7: *Velox Waterways* by William Schooner

Chapter 5

Along the River Crease

Upstream from the capital city, Veloxeter, the River Crease meanders slowly through the water meadows and pastures of the provinces of Velox and Campana. Many barges ply up and down the river transporting grain, timber, wool and stone. The old eighteenth-century towpaths and sluices are still preserved in the middle reaches of the river, making it possible to walk along most of the Crease between March and Hubcaster. A fast cycleway snakes along the southern side of the river while the northern bank is followed by the main electric train line. The river is a popular for rowing, the annual Campana versus Velox race towards the lower reaches of the Crease as it enters Veloxeter being the Dynamoan equivalent of the Oxford versus Cambridge race on the Thames in London.

The River Crease marks the boundary between the two provinces, separating the lake-lands of Velox to the north from the drier arable fields of Campana to the south. The Willow Lakes are enjoyed not only for their unspoilt natural beauty, their plentiful fish and wildfowl, but also as a place for water sport. It is a common sight therefore to see yachts apparently sailing across the countryside, as the shallow broads and river bends of the Willow Lakes and tributaries of the Crease provide waterways through the fen and carr that characterise the region. The abundant reeds harvested give rise to a thatch industry that still thrives as the old vernacular style of building and roofing persists into the twenty-first century.

The province of Velox is also home to the Dynamo cricketing tradition, with the country's most famous club (the March

Cricket Club or MCC) established at March, the regional capital. The approach to March is particularly spectacular as its medieval cathedral, built on an island on a broad bend in the river, appears to row with its flying buttresses towards approaching craft. The many willow trees that line the river banks (the willow is the symbol of the province) and lakeshore provide the wood for cricket bats while the leather used in the manufacture of cricket balls comes from the cattle-rearing plains of Campana, south of the river. March is also an important railway junction on the main west-east line connecting Veloxeter to Hubcaster and the upland towns of Upper March, Top March, Oarhouse and Rugby. The name 'March' derives from the 'Marches' that punctuated the Roman armies' third-century progress up the River Crease from Veloxeter.

The province of Campana is the breadbasket of Dynamo, its level plains producing rich harvests of wheat, barley, sugar-beat and potatoes. The attractive seaside town of Louisville, in the east, famous for its football club the Louisville Wanderers and for its race-course, is the centre of a market-gardening area that provides the capital Veloxeter with fruit and vegetables. Georgia, Louisville's twin, situated on the coast just north of the capital in Velox Province, is an elegant spa town, famous for its eighteenth-century seaside terraces and its opulent pleasure gardens. It is probably the most fashionable town in the country, the Dynamoan equivalent of Brighton.

Chapter 6

History

Before the arrival of the Celts in 1000 BC, Dynamo was, like the more westerly parts of Europe, uninhabited. But when humans did arrive, the presence of gold and base metals in the Handlebar Mountains and the fertile eastern plains facilitated the rapid establishment of human culture, attested to today by the large number of Celtic burial sites and archaeological remains. The meeting of the mountains and the plains in the level foothills east of the Handlebar range was the site of particularly rich cultural development, with a major religious and ceremonial site, Marl Grange, at the meeting of the rivers Rafter and Crease in the region of Lower March and Hubcaster. Since there were no natives on the island prior to the Celts, the latter were able to develop a rich and homogeneous culture.

Dynamo Island was in turn discovered by the Romans at the time of Hadrian's rule (second century AD). Roman ships en route for Britannia had been blown off course and managed to make landfall in the southern part of the island. Realising the rich potential of what they had discovered, the Romans quickly established a capital at Hadrianopolis, at the mouth of the river Antinous, named by Hadrian himself after his favourite, on a visit to the island on a return trip from Britannia. The resistance of the native Celts, or *Velociae* as the Romans called them, was fierce. Fleet of foot and with hard and dexterous hands, the Velociae were formidable opponents in hand-to-hand battle and on horse-back. Celtic resistance was particularly strong in the southern regions first discovered by the Romans and in particular in the province centred on the Ring Mountains that

Hadrian named Pugilia. A major victory of the Romans at the Celtic regional capital of Boxcaster (*Buxus castra*) on the River Antinous however marked the first stage of Roman occupation of the island.

The Celtic prowess in the martial arts meant that, when finally subdued, they became prized within the Roman Empire as boxers, gladiators and charioteers. Amphitheatres were quickly established at Hadrianopolis and Boxcaster, and later at Hubcaster and Veloxeter. The level plains of the eastern side of the island and the broad valleys of the River Crease's many tributaries facilitated the construction of paved roads enabling Roman troops to establish their dominance in the southern, eastern and northern parts of the island. As in Britannia, the Celtic strongholds retreated to the western mountains where they managed to survive despite many punitive expeditions on the part of the Romans. A famous battle at Rory Gap in 300 AD at which Celtic defenders inflicted serious losses on Roman troops marks the beginning of the decline of Roman power in the island. However two generations of intermarriage between Romans and Celts, the establishment of Latin as the dominant language and the installation of Roman-style infrastructures resulted in the convergence, as in Britannia, of the two racial and cultural traditions to form a new synthesis.

Apart from the establishment of towns and roads, baths and amphitheatres, the cult of games and martial sports, the Romans also built up trade links with other parts of the Empire, in particular through the eastern and subsequently national capital of Veloxeter. They also diversified the island's agriculture, planting vines in the southeast and introducing many Mediterranean herbs and shrubs. Roman mythology merged with or superseded Celtic religious beliefs, with a particularly rich synthesis of rituals relating to monthly and seasonal cycles. The

8. Roman Amphitheatre, Boxcaster

Roman calendar was adopted, along with the Roman system of measurements and currency. Early Velocian coinage displays the Wheel, subsequently to become the country's national symbol, with, on its obverse, profiles of successive Roman emperors.

Like Britain in the seventh and eighth centuries, Dynamo was visited and settled by Angles, Saxons and Jutes. The prevailing Latin tongue became anglicised and with the coming of Christianity in the ninth century, established by St David, the island's culture became progressively Europeanised. Periodic incursions and subsequent settlement by the Vikings and the Normans in the tenth and eleventh centuries further diversified the island's linguistic and cultural traditions. Ownership of the land, established by the Romans on an individual as opposed to tribal basis, was continued: although there were some large estates that later became the basis of a landed aristocracy, the general pattern was one of smaller estates owned by individual farming families, with common land and grazing rights for all villages. Although certain powerful regional chieftains had in the ninth and tenth centuries attempted to establish themselves as national monarchs, the strong tradition of regional independence prevailing in the eight Roman-founded provinces, meant that no legitimate monarchy was ever established. Instead was inaugurated a system whereby the heads of the eight provinces met at regular intervals of the year at Hubcaster, the old capital, to agree national policy. Disagreements between the eight chiefs, who nominated on an annual basis one of their number as presider-in-chief, were resolved by referring issues to the vote of all land-owners (possessing more than one acre) and house-holding citizens of the towns. In this way, a tradition of broad, if often painfully slow, consensus was established in the island.

The power of the Church in Dynamo was curtailed in a similar way to that in Britain, the country becoming by the seventeenth century a protestant Commonwealth on the model of what Cromwell had already attempted to establish in Britain. The later seventeenth century marked Dynamo's first golden age, with the establishment of an Academy of Sciences, of universities in Veloxeter, Hubcaster, Rugby and Upper March, with a naval college at Hadrianopolis. The new, more fully representative, parliament was established in a magnificent new building in Veloxeter with an upper house consisting of representatives of each of the eight provinces, each of whom was to be over 50 years of age, with women as well as men being eligible for election. Each of the eight provinces had its capital city with a regional council that enacted legislation of the national government and dealt with local affairs. The distinctive qualities and characteristics of the regions were jealously guarded with a strong tradition of friendly rivalry between them. Inspired by the model of the United States of America, in the late eighteenth century

Dynamo adopted a fully representative democratic political system with a written constitution and a Bill of Human Rights. The capital of the country at Veloxeter became the country's chief administrative centre. The House of Representatives was elected by all adults, male and female, of 21 years and over, the Upper House or Senate consisting of thirty-two senior citizens – sixteen men, sixteen women – also elected by general consensus. From the time of the Napoleonic wars, the country adopted a policy of neutrality. Its strong navy protected its shores and maritime routes while its army was trained for national defence rather than expeditionary engagement abroad.

Despite its strategic position in the mid-Atlantic, during both World War I and World War II, Dynamo was able to maintain its neutrality. It was beyond the range of German bombers in World War II and well south of the main north-Atlantic convoy routes between America and Britain. It was nevertheless on full alert during both world wars and its merchant and naval fleets were instructed to save survivors of torpedoed allied shipping. During the Cold War period of the second half of the twentieth century, Dynamo became a member of the North Atlantic Treaty Organisation (NATO) and entered the European Community (EU) in the early 1970s, at the same time as Britain and Ireland. It now takes very seriously its integration into the European Union, in which its influence has been strongly felt in particular in relation to human rights and environmental issues.

9: *Olympia Countryside* **by Paul Mash**

Chapter 7

The Vales of Olympia

Bounded in the northwest by the River Rafter and the south-east by the Antinous, the Province of Olympia consists in the eastern half of a broad limestone plains and in the west and south of the Handlebar mountains. Its rich, mixed deciduous and pine forests provide an abundance of timber that provides raw material for the paper and construction industries of Oarhouse, capital of Spokane, at the confluence of the Oar and the Rafter. The Handlebar Mountains are also rich in gold, silver and other valuable metals, leading to important specialised industries in Odessa, the capital city, including precision engineering and jewellery. Odessa, is situated at the edge of a beautiful lake, in a natural arena at the foot of the Handlebar range. The city is also the site of a number of spas that were developed from Roman times on the basis of mineral springs that rose from the foothills of the Handlebar Mountains. In the eighteenth century, Odessa was therefore the Bath or Buxton of Dynamo, sharing with those cities an elegant neo-classical architectural style that was adapted to street-planning, often in the form of circuses, crescents as well as to the principal municipal buildings and fashionable centres of entertainment such as the Assembly Rooms, the Opera and the Theatre. The honey-coloured local stone was widely used and, indeed, to this day predominates as a building material in the centre of the city, though some major recent architectural projects provide a contrast with their gleaming white ceramic façades. The most famous of these is the Odessa Opera House: situated at the edge of the lake, the four majestic sail-like motifs that decorate its skyline resemble the profile of traditional Olympian watercraft.

10: View of Odessa

Odessa is also the home of one of Dynamo's most famous universities, George Hagel College (named in honour of the province's
greatest philosopher), situated in a former eighteenth-century
mansion in a splendid setting just outside the city. Its
government- and industry-funding make it one of the country's
leading research institutions, with many important specialised
high-tech industrial developments situated around it. The city is
also home to the country's leading sports college, Ashford Forum,
which plays an important role in making the country one of the
leaders in athletics (track and field) in the European community.
Ash-keys are the province's symbol and figure prominently in the
College's badge.

The province's eastern plains are not only important for arable
agriculture (wheat, barley, sugar-beat, potatoes) but also as a
military training ground: a large area west of Boxcaster at
Infantry Plain is designated for army training while the main air-

force training base in the country is sited at Skybourne just south of Lower March. The Dynamoan air force is primarily defensive in its role, with squadrons of interceptor aircraft stationed at strategic points in the country, the main base being near Boxcaster. There are also shipboard fighters flown by the Dynamoan Navy, whose operations are coordinated with other NATO forces. For ecological reasons, Dynamo has kept internal flying to a minimum, though the international airports at Veloxeter and Hubcaster are always busy and constitute the home bases of the national airline, Aero Dynamo.

11: Aero Dynamo airline logo

Chapter 8

Politics and Institutions

The dominant principle governing the ethos of Dynamo is that man and the animal kingdom are the centre of the world and that as far as possible all infrastructure and activity should be scaled appropriately. So, for example, the straw-bales produced on farms are lift-able by the average human and the vast machine-produced and fork-lift handled bales of modern Europe and America that disfigure the landscape by their inappropriate scale and their black plastic covering are not to be seen. Similarly, all buildings outside the larger cities are restricted to two or three stories and natural lighting is a top priority in all architectural design. Much importance is attached to the relationship between inside and outside, with arcades, verandas and other sorts of spaces between interior and exterior being maximally valued. Humans are as far as possible encouraged to use their own powers of movement – walking, cycling, sailing – with use of public transport for longer distances. The banishment of the motor vehicle, whether private or utilitarian, has massively facil-itated this. The continued use of animals – horses, ponies, even oxen – for light or heavy transport in the countryside enhances both human understanding of and sympathy with the animal kingdom and the well-being of the ecological system.

This ethos of human scale and purpose extends to the democ-ratic principles underlying the Republic's political structures. The federal republican system means that inhabitants of each of the eight provinces are fully aware of the issues that are important to them and feel they have a real influence on how they are dealt with through the regional parliaments. Communal participation in sports and leisure activities and the public funding of all major facilities means that every citizen feels they have a stake in the country and that their voice can be heard. Motivation to excel, to work hard and to prosper is provided by a competitive streak in the national ethos which is fuelled by regional, sporting and other competitions and by the wish on the part of most people to demonstrate their physical, social and intellectual skills by performing well in whatever activity they engage in. Traditional skills (printing, weaving, wood-carving) are highly prized while new technologies (electronics, computers, visual media, telecommunications) are taught in all second-level schools and regional colleges. The older generations are valued for their experience and skills, while their generally high level of fitness and mental alertness means that they continue to contribute vitally to the life of the community.

The general appreciation of the importance of good health and exercise means that the country's national health system is able to operate efficiently and democratically without crippling internal finances. The ethos of physical and sporting activities, and the absence of smog, mean that the incidence of heart and lung disease is low, whilst the relatively slower productivity rate of a zero-growth economy means there is less stress. Pleasure is taken in as many aspects as possible of human and natural life, with cooking, eating, gardening, caring for animals and plants all integrated as pleasurable as well as essential aspects of everyday life. All children brought up in cities are invited to spend at least two weeks of the year living and working in the country, with country children similarly spending part of their holidays in the cities. The extension on a national scale of media technology to the remotest towns means that people living in remote areas do not feel deprived of the stimulus the city can offer. The notion that human economies produce waste for recycling rather than rubbish means that people have a higher appreciation of the value of materials and the excitement of transforming 'waste' into new materials or products is discovered to be as vital as is the case with raw materials.

The national commitment to openness and transparency in public and political life is reflected in the architecture of civic and governmental buildings. Like the government buildings and chancellery in modern Berlin, the new Parliament building in Dynamo's capital, Veloxeter, is constructed across the meanders of the River Crease about a mile upstream from where it disgorges its waters into the Atlantic Ocean. The sides of the buildings are mostly glazed from ground level to rooftop with various openings into courts and squares that give air and breathing space. As in Berlin, public walkways pass through the buildings at street level while river transport passes beneath the buildings along the Crease. Large works of contemporary painting and sculpture are mounted in these buildings in such a way as to both enhance their visibility to the public and enrich the aesthetic impact of the setting. The elected Upper House of the Dynamo governmental system sits in an oval pink granite building sited in one of Veloxeter's main parks. Its entrance incorporates a discreet but legible digital notice board that informs the public of the names of Upper House representatives present within the building and the programme of debates scheduled for the day. Each of the main ministry buildings in the capital city is equipped with a similar display system showing the names of the minister and senior staff and providing a brief outline of the ministry's function, while the country's written constitution and the bill of human rights are engraved in gold letters in the wall of the national parliament building.

Since there are no motorcars in Dynamo, there are no ministerial limousines; members of Parliament, the Upper House and ministers travel about the city in small electric taxis, painted in the national colours of green and blue, to distinguish them from the otherwise similar public taxis painted in grey. It is not unusual to see ministers and members of Parliament traveling round the city by bike. On state occasions, the president is driven in a horse-drawn carriage dating back two centuries with a ceremonial guard mounted on horseback. The annual opening of each parliamentary session is marked by a boat-trip down the river Crease to the Parliament buildings, in which all elected members participate. This ceremony marks a long tradition according to which elected representatives of seven of Dynamo's eight federal states used to travel by boat down the Crease and its various tributaries to take their seats in the national parliament at Veloxeter. Representatives from the eighth state, Maurice Island, came by sea to Veloxeter from Quinnport to rejoin their fellows from the other states.

Dynamo's national ethos finds its clearest expression in the national flag, established with the Republic's new constitution in the late eighteenth century. Consisting of a wheel centred in an oblong divided horizontally, the lower half green and the upper half blue, the flag symbolizes the harmony of natural elements and the necessity of ecological balance between climate and sky and land and sea. The white central wheel is divided into eight equal sections, representing the balance and equilibrium that unites the Republic's eight provinces. The incorporation of the blue top part of the flag into the green bottom half of the central hemisphere and the reciprocal presence of the colour green into the upper half of reflects the ethos of re-cycling and reciprocal accord central to Dynamo.

12: Government buildings, Veloxeter (architect: Henry Scott)

Chapter 9

Picturesque Hubcaster

At the confluence of the River Pitch and the River Crease, at the highest navigation point of the latter, and marking the site where the eight provinces of Dynamo meet, Hubcaster is in every sense the country's central city. Its industries – milling, brewing, agricultural and railway engineering, wool and linen – also make it the country's second largest manufacturing town. Until the eighteenth century the country's capital city and centre of the profitable wool-trade, Hubcaster has long been an important cultural centre with the finest medieval town centre in the country. The city's location, where the limestone plateaux of the west pass underneath a stratum of chalk, means that flint (associated with calcareous deposits) was always plentiful, leading both to the surrounding area's importance in Stone-Age times and also, from the Middle Ages, ensuring a plentiful supply of flint for building. Hubcaster's cityscape is therefore a maze of brick-and-flint buildings, from the old Guild Hall to the Mansion House and the former Parliament building, now the regional assembly house of the province of Arcadia. The confluence of the rivers, together with the importance of river transport (for grain, wool, timber and other building materials), together with many local interconnecting creeks and canals, mean that the city seems like one built on water, with many of the old red-brick mills and warehouses backing onto the waterways that supplied them with raw materials.

The famous Hubcaster School of Painting, with its masters such as John Chrome and John Spell, provides a picturesque record of the cityscape of the late eighteenth- and early nineteenth-century golden age, with their paintings of the city gates, the timber-yards and warehouses, the old sun-warmed brick walls of the mill-yards, whose bases are lapped by the waters of the Pitch or the Crease and where working men, breeches and shirt-sleeves rolled, fished or waded in the warm shallows. The historic market place, framed by the Guild Hall, the Mansion House, the old Parliament Building and St Peter's Church, has for centuries provided the focus of the city's trade and commerce, offering for sale produce and manufactures from the eight province of Dynamo. The twelfth-century Cathedral, with its tall and graceful spire, is the landmark of the lower reaches of the city; its elegant Close is surrounded by the willows and water-meadows that characterise the Crease from this point downstream, a landscape also lovingly explored by painters of the Hubcaster School.

13: *Back of Old Mills, Hubcaster, men wading* **by John Chrome**

Chapter 10

Cultural and Artistic Traditions

From the seventeenth century up until the modern period, the dominant preoccupations in the visual arts have been landscape, portrait and genre painting. The great seventeenth-century neoclassical painter Edward Persil was the last in Dynamo to give vigorous expression to mythology in a landscape setting somewhat in the manner of Poussin in France. With the eighteenth century Henry Woodcock (genre), Thomas Flamborough (portraiture) and George Strobe (equestrian subjects) established their pre-eminence in these genres. Woodcock's paintings of the romantic scenery of the Ring Mountains are particularly prized, as are the landscapes of the Hubcaster School (late eighteenth- and early nineteenth-century), in particular those of John Chrome and John Spell. In the later nineteenth century, the wild scenery of the Handlebar Mountains and the bucolic serenity of Arcadia found expression in the impressionist works of Alfred Sizzler. In the early nineteenth century, Albert Spinks in his famous etchings and lithographs of boxers, jockeys and other sportsmen brought the art of the sporting print to perfection, a tradition developed later in the century by Wholesale Hunt and Gilbert Guy who brought the representation of contemporary urban life to a new level of sophistication and irony. As befits an island, there are several major painters of the sea, most notably the Maurice Island artists William Schooner and Edwin Hulk, whose subtle translucency of colour verges on abstraction.

In the twentieth century, the landscape tradition with a strong feeling for the local and the vernacular was continued in the work of artists such as Eric Ravisher and Paul Mash, while the combination of topographical sensitivity and formal abstraction was brought to a new level of perfection in the work of Ivan Lichen whose wide landscape-format compositions make him the major Dynamoan artist of the first half of the twentieth century. European-style modernism had a muted impact on Dynamoan artistic tradition, though the profound influence of Fernand Léger and the Italian Futurists is very evident in modern Dynamoan graphic design. The representation of speed, industrial activity and technological development is manifest in the work of the Spartan artist Fortunato Desperado while a reflection on the factitiousness of modern culture and the image in consumer society is evident in the work of the Veloxeter School Pop artists such as Andy Soapbox and Ray Flashback. In the postmodern era, Dynamoan artists struggle to respond to the global world while maintaining authentic contact with the island's traditional visual culture. The Museum of Modern Art in Veloxeter (MOMAV) has one of the finest collections of paintings of the twentieth century and organises an important biennial international exhibition of contemporary art, while Hubcaster is the home of the National Gallery of Art, showcasing in particular Dynamoan painting from the seventeenth to the nineteenth century.

14: *Headwaters of the River Crease* **by John Spell**

Chapter 11

The Plains of Campana

The plains of Campana probably do not look very different from the time of the Roman occupation of Dynamo: broad arable plains covered in fields of wheat and barley bordered by shimmering avenues of poplars and plane trees and clumps of laurel (the symbol of the province). The straight Roman roads connect regularly spaced nucleated settlements, still very often rectilinear in plan. The two-lane cycle paths, standard throughout Dynamo Island, follow these main routes so that it is possible to cover many miles quickly and safely. Many of the farmsteads follow the Roman pattern, being built round a central court or farmyard, three sides of which is occupied by cattle-sheds, grain-stores and plough-sheds, with the fourth constituting the farmhouse. Water towers and wind pumps add a curiously Australian touch to the landscape. There are also many orchards and fields of hops, with town-dwellers traditionally spending part of their summer working as fruit- or hop-pickers in the countryside. The eastern parts of the province in particular are covered in market gardens that supply fresh fruit and vegetables for Louisville and the capital, Veloxeter.

Cattle-ranching also contributes a major part of Campana's economy, with leather and leather goods as well as beef being important products. Campana leather is used in all kinds of sports gear from cricket balls to saddlery. Horse-rearing is also an important activity of the province. The racecourse at Louisville is the most important in the country, the annual Louisville Cup being the Dynamoan equivalent of Cheltenham Races or the Derby. The fame of the honey-coloured horses of Campana from the eighteenth century is attested to not only by the many famous stables and stud farms scattered over the province but also by one of the greater painters of Dynamo, George Strobe, whose equestrian subjects are in high demand.

The white chalk cliffs of Campana that stretch in an almost unbroken line from Louisville to Anasi Point shelter popular holiday beaches and small fishing ports, though Louisville and Anasi, at either extremity, are the main resort towns. Anasi, an important brewing and fish-processing centre, is the state capital. It is a famous gastronomic centre, drawing its wide range of cuisines from the varied produce of the Campana Plains and also the vines (introduced by the Romans) that grow on the south-facing cliffs to the east of the city. Nestling at the foot of the dramatic promontory of Anasi Point, the city marks the end of the plains and the abrupt rise of the Ring Mountains that surge upwards to the west to a height of 3000 feet.

Anasi is the most Italianate of Dynamo's cities, its old town centre, sited on a steep rise above the coast, being bejewelled with seventeenth- and eighteenth-century churches. Some of the picturesque houses that cluster in the narrow and irregular pedestrian streets today accommodate the restaurants that make Anasi the gastronomic capital of the country. The famous film studios are sited on the eastern outskirts of the city and overlook the blue expanse of the Atlantic Ocean.

15: *Campana Farmhouse* **by Ivan Lichen**

Chapter 12

Literature and Philosophy

The eight regional universities of the Federal republic of Dynamo reflect in their names the eight philosophers who have shaped Dynamoan thinking since the seventeenth century: Jake Russet (Arcadia), Charles Derwent (Campana), Alfred Onestone (Maurice Island), George Hagel (Olympia), Frederick Netshow (Pugilia), Charles Symbol Purse (Sparta), Jack Derider (Spokane) and Blair Pastel (Velox County). Deeply attached to the physical recalcitrance of their homeland – a rugged island in a vast sea with high mountains and fertile plains – Dynamoans have always been deeply suspicious of metaphysics. Profoundly shaped by their ancient pantheistic beliefs, their deities were first and foremost related to the material aspect of the world, only secondarily as agents inspiring spiritual or conceptual values.

Their great seventeenth-century philosopher, Blair Pastel, gave modern expression to this outlook with his conception of the rational element as being only one aspect of human mental make-up and his affirmation that knowledge was acquired also through the senses (through scientific observation), the emotions (moral and aesthetics values) and through belief – whether in a deity or in the first principles on which conceptions, language and law were based. This view was amplified in the eighteenth century by Russet who, like European thinkers of this period, stressed the importance of subjective desire in human knowledge and belief, and emphasised the creative role of the imagination as both a synthesising and an analytical agent. This intuition was subsequently submitted by George Hagel, at the beginning of the nineteenth century, to a systematic analysis in which the dialec-

47

tical relation between spirit and matter was argued for, establishing a plausible model of the way the mind absorbs, transforms and yet still retains elements of the material or sensual world it both institutes and undergoes.

The power of matter as a fundamentally irrational and self-transforming agent was radically demonstrated in the field of biology by Charles Derwent who showed that the millions of species that constitute the natural world survive purely according to the chance adaptation of some of them to their environment, these species, over time, tending to survive where others die off. Twentieth-century understanding of the genetic process in biological development would confirm aspects of Derwent's evolutionary thesis. At about the same time, in the realm of philosophy, the radical and eccentric figure of Netshow was to demonstrate that religion, philosophy and morality were equally arbitrary as values or constructions of the human mind, and that the values that would ultimately prevail would be those most in tune with a will to survive, fully in the knowledge that there was no absolute necessity for them, or indeed for human life. Netshow's critical interrogation of language was shared by another great Dynamoan, Charles Symbol Purse, who established that the ultimate real of matter and feeling was probably unknowable since humans could only communicate – knowledge, sentiment, belief – through *representation*. Thus semiology, drawing on the insights of Hagen and Netshow, became an established discipline within the human sciences.

In mathematics and physics, the question of the relationship between matter and the dynamic principles operative in the universe – energy, movement, time – was radically clarified by Alfred Onestone who in a celebrated algebraic formula showed that time, space and energy were all part of a homogeneous complex whose apparently different manifestations were merely a function of the relative position from which they were viewed: once again, as with Derwent, the human position was viewed as being a chance development, inadequate to grasping let alone commanding the situation in which it found itself. In the realm of language and philosophy, the great late twentieth-century thinker Jack Derider, elaborated this principle in relation to writing, which he showed to have no logical beginning or end, to be constantly in a state of movement and transformation, and yet beyond which it was impossible to move since humankind is condemned to inhabit an epistemological world of symbolic (mis-)representation.

As a result of this, twenty-first-century Dynamoans broadly share a belief in their existence in an irrational world, one that has no organising principle other than that of chance and the laws of physics – insofar as these latter may be construed to be knowable. This realistic appraisal of existence has not led to nihilism or despair, but, on the contrary, to an enthusiastic acceptance of existence as it is offered to humankind and to a commitment to understanding and enjoying the miracle of it to the fullest degree. The fact that the beauty of the rose is purely a matter of chance, and that symmetries in human appearance or in their artistic creations have no intrinsic meaning, does not prevent the estimation and celebration of these phenomena. There is therefore a strong element of Epicureanism in the Dynamoan philosophy, coupled with a marked sense of community: since all humans depend on each other to survive within it, Dynamoans celebrate their shared fate and the beautiful if irrational environment in which they evolved. This does not mean that Dynamoans give themselves up passively to the destiny which has been meted out to them, but on the contrary they strive constantly to question and interrogate the physical and moral laws of their universe, seeking no final or absolute solution to the problems it poses, but merely endeavouring to enhance their understanding, and therefore acceptance, of it.

16: *View of Anasi* **by Henry Woodcock**

The integration of the human and the natural world that is intrinsic to the Dynamoan cultural tradition is reflected in the country's literary tradition. Although, since the time of the Romans, European classicism has strongly marked Dynamo's culture, the country has also always, like England, exhibited strong Romantic tendencies in which powerful individual or communal feelings of interaction with the natural world have led to an organic and imaginative approach to literary creation. The strong pantheistic tendencies of the country, along with the continuing vitality of local traditions and mythologies, have resulted in a highly imaged and sensuous poetry. In drama, the pre-eminence of comedy perhaps reflects the humorous acceptance of difference nurtured within a country with strong regional variations in customs and traditions. The national poet, William Bird, like Shakespeare in England, combines in his poetry and his plays (mostly comedies) a powerful lyrical propensity with brilliant and witty wordplay. The epic tradition, vital in the seventeenth and eighteenth centuries, gives expression to the conflict between Romano-European influxes from around AD 200 and the older Celtic traditions of the preceding half millennium. Whereas in Britain Miltonic epic was magisterially synthesising Christian and Classical mythology, in the work of Dynamo's great epic poet, Gilbert Moth, the fusion of Roman and modern mythologies came to the fore. The country's greatest lyric poets, Andrew Wonder and John Donwell, writing in the seventeenth century, explored the tensions between urban and civic values and those of a more traditional rural and pastoral tradition, a preoccupation renewed and rejuvenated in the nineteenth century by Romantic poets such as Robert Rose and Patrick Horizon. The following poem, written by the latter, a native of Arcadia, gives an idea:

A Song of Rural Obscurity

Out of the thicket a bird – a partridge
Beats its wings laboriously into flight
In a heavy diagonal climb cross the furrows.
Under the bank, through the hemlock and mallow,
A rabbit bobs towards the burrows of the warren.
A sparrow flits through the orchard's
Fawn confusion to the barn:
Oak beams bending under a heavy sky;
Thatch collapsing beneath
Invisible pigeons' insidious cooing.
Guttering hanging precariously over

The lichened timbers of a decaying water butt
Cracking like nut, hollow of kernel.
A broken ladder's rungs climb to a vacant gable.
A gate swings open into a barren yard;
Windows blinded with ivy through a long absence of eyes
Squint from inscrutable brickwork,
Whilst through a warped frame a blank doorway gapes.

Grass grows out of the hayrick's hat
And moss is carpeting the scullery;
The clatter in the dairy is caused by the rat
And the loft is the bat's dark gallery.

What trace remains here of a human domain?
What consciousness lurks among the cracks in the plaster?
Whose eyes observe this leisurely disaster?
Is there an old man snoring in a ditch of vetch and dandelion
Who will wake and relate the history of hereabouts?
Or is the mystery sealed
In the hieroglyphs of wheeling birds forever?

The fragmentation and cultural diversity that characterise European and American modernism is also present in twentieth-century Dynamo culture in which the generically problematic texts of poets such as Alexander Box and David Detroit explore the complex interaction of different linguistic and cultural traditions. Their (respective) poems *Walking round the Square* (1922) and *In the Boxing Ring* (1936) express the profound tension in modern life between rationalist symmetry and irrational urges, the Apollonian and the Dionysiac, the intellectual and the visceral, as in the following poem:

Unidentified Boxer

Whose is the body, identified only
By a gum-shield grimace,
Lolling rapturously backwards,
Gloved fists helplessly akimbo,
Limbo-dancing to oblivion
Across the ice-rink of the canvas?
His is the dream and the nightmare
Of every man of average mettle
Channelling intermittent currents
Of fantasy and adrenaline
Into the alluring danger of the ring
Where a camera's black box flash
Captures with a shutter's snap
The slow rush to unconsciousness.

The question of national identity in the face of immigration and globalisation is an important theme in later twentieth-century writing, as in Kevin Kapor's highly acclaimed novels *Strangers to Ourselves* (1984) and *Vive la différence* (1998). Women writers have played a central role in the development of literature in Dynamo since the seventeenth century, with Emily House (*Duty Calls*, 1666), Charlotte Craft (*Marriage à la mode*, 1792), Isabella Strand (*Home Truths*, 1854) and Flora Dine (*The Matchmaker*, 1924) in successive centuries exploring the changing roles of women in the domestic and public spheres. In the 1950s and 60s, the Modern Crisis movement of post-war poets was concerned to explore the moral and political issues at stake in relation to the catastrophes of twentieth-century history, in particular the Second World War – as in David Mark's poem which strives to engage with the moral and philosophical ambiguity of the contemporary position:

At Todtnauberg (some time) after Paul Celan

Colt's-foot, windflower
We follow dubious
Directions
Among tracks still snow-bordered
On the *schattenseite*

And approach the *hütte*
From behind

We try to see the view
– Fir-lined ridges against further ridges –
As Heidegger might have

But much intervenes

– New buildings, ski-lifts, old prejudices –

The draft from the well with the
Star-die on top
Is still pure

The air is still pure

And the hope, today,
For a thinker's word
To come in the heart

But being (knowing, judging)

– Despite snow hieroglyphs on the north-facing slopes –

Is still
like a rock-fall.

17: *Metal Workshops, Rugby* by **Fortunato Desperado**

Chapter 13

Industrial Sparta

Sparta is the largest province of Dynamo Island and the most intensively industrialised. The region between Rugby on the River Pitch, and Top March, Upper March and Lower March on the River Wicket, is the most densely populated part of the country with a wide range of manufacturing and processing industries. The existence of large iron ore deposits, and some coal, in the limestone escarpments and of lead, zinc, copper and gold in the Handlebar Mountains, led from the late eighteenth century to an important metallurgical industry, one that with modernisation and refinement has continued to thrive until today. Rugby's city centre is still an attractive jumble of late eighteenth- and early nineteenth-century metal workshops, many of which are still active, and is criss-crossed by an old narrow-gauge railway that continues to provide essential transport for raw materials and finished products between the various workshops and depots of the city. While Rugby from the beginning of the railway age in the early nineteenth century became the country's leading producer of steel rails, bridging, cranes and dockland winches, nearly two hundred years later Lower March, at the confluence of the Crease and the Rafter, is the centre of engineering (machine tools, factory robotics, electric motors) and is famous for its Dynamo Institute of Technology (DIT).

Upper March is famous for its ceramic and glass industries, using local clay and sand, while Top March specialises in high-quality clockwork, camera and other optical equipment. 'Wicket' watches are prized throughout the country, while 'Top March' digital cameras are an important export. Significant dying and chemical industries are established at Lower March, using the abundant waters of the converging tributaries of the Crease and the local potash deposits. Hydroelectric stations towards the headwaters of these tributaries provide the energy to power not only the region's industry but also the bulk of the country's electric train system. The more recent development of wind- and wave-power is centred at Philadelpho and New Dublin on the north coast of Sparta, which is itself the choice site of these energy-producing installations as it is exposed to Atlantic winds and tides. Philadelpho is also an important port for coal and other raw material imports and for export of Spartan industrial goods.

The rugged nature of Spartan scenery, particularly the hills to the west, is reflected in the proverbial strength and resistance of the natives. Sparta is the home of Dynamoan rugby (the province's badge is the rugby pine), with the various March towns, along with Rugby, Philadelpho and Oarhouse (in Spokane) engaging in strong regional sporting rivalries. The tough resistance of the Celtic tribes to Roman invasion meant that for several centuries there were violent skirmishes between the two, though the famous repulsion of the Roman legionaries by the Celtic chieftain, Rory, at Rory Gap in 300AD, marked the end of Roman domination and the start of a progressive unifying of the different traditions. Owing to its gold deposits and, further east, the outcrops of flint, the high limestone plains of Sparta and Spokane were the site of a pre-historic civilisation, whose most famous monument is the 3000-year-old stone henge situated at Marl Grange, at the confluence of the rivers Rafter and Crease. Aligned on a north-south axis, it seems to have had both religious and astrological functions.

18: Dynamo Rails, Dynamo Trams – company logos

Chapter 14

Industry, Economy, Commerce

The national aim of Dynamo – to sustain near full employment and general prosperity on the basis of zero economic growth – is one that has been largely achieved through careful balancing of productivity and environmental demands. The country's exports and imports are largely balanced. This is made possible by the country's self-sufficiency in food and its economy's minimal dependence on oil. Exports are high-quality agricultural goods, machinery, electronic goods, wood and paper products, sports equipment, textiles; imports are raw materials (especially metals), coal, aircraft fuel. The economy is about 500 billion Euros. Huge energy savings are possible since there is no motor transport and thus little use of oil. Recycling is a major industry and employer. National and regional projects are instigated if unemployment reaches higher than 5%. The gap between rich and poor is kept as narrow as possible. Since the 1960s, 80% taxation has been instituted for those earning more than €250,000 per annum. Taxation is high in all income categories but compensated by heavy state subsidies on health, education, transport and social welfare. Owing to the strict controls on financial dealings, the crisis that devastated the economies of the western world after 2008 was largely avoided. The main banks are national-owned and strictly regulated, with a rigid separation between savings and investment. The Veloxeter stock exchange is relatively small since speculation is less part of the economic ethos of Dynamo than is the case in other western countries. The desire to acquire inordinate wealth is generally frowned upon since the Dynamo ethos is centred on preserving the environment and a healthy, balanced life-style. Since there are no cars or private planes and private ownership is restricted to a maximum of two properties, scope for conspicuous consumption or display of wealth is markedly reduced. As a member of the EU and the Euro, Dynamo is subject to the same legislation on labour movement and budget restrictions as other European countries.

Chapter 15

The Handlebar Mountains

Forming a more or less equilateral triangle marked by the River Wicket to the north and the Rafter to the south, Spokane is Dynamo's most mountainous province, boasting the country's highest peak, Mount David, which rises to over 5000 feet. The western wall of the Handlebar Mountains is so impenetrable that the main east-west railway line from Lower March to Gary Head, on Dynamo's western coast, has at its western extremity to burrow through a long tunnel. Before the railway was built, traffic had to cross the mountain peaks by the Connor Pass, 50km upstream from Rory Gap in the Crease valley, a route that in bad winters was often closed by snow. The upper tributaries of the Crease cut deep valleys into the mountains that, in winter, become popular skiing resorts, with Rory Gap becoming the country's centre for winter sports. Toboggan courses there are among the most hair-raising in the world. The pure waters, pellucid mountain air and lush pastures of the lower slopes of the Handlebars make this area, like the European Alps, a favourite place for hiking and rambling in the summer, activities much promoted among all ages in Dynamo, providing an accessible outlet to the populous industrial towns of neighbouring Sparta. The coastal towns situated on Spokane's western seaboard – St Sebastian and Gary Head (like Cliveden, further north in Sparta) – are major fishing ports with many canning and fish-processing factories. The coasts are famous for their shellfish and their many excellent seafood restaurants. Fresh oysters and mussels as well as fish are sent daily by rail eastwards via Hubcaster to Veloxeter, 450km away.

The province's capital, Oarhouse, is a major industrial town, specialising in electric locomotives and boatbuilding. Surrounded by rich pine and deciduous forests, it is also the centre of the country's paper-milling and furniture industries, with an important college of industrial design. It is also a pioneer in the re-cycling industry, managing to maintain an 80% re-use rate of discarded materials. Situated at the confluence of the Oar and the Rafter, Oarhouse is one of the most elegantly planned of Dynamo's capital cities. Devastated by a fire in 1950 that started in a bakery and then swept through the city, burning many of its traditional wooden houses, the city was rebuilt by the corporation in such a way as to maximise the harmonious juxtaposition of industrial activity and civic and residential amenities. Luckily, some of the old brick warehouses that line the rivers Oar and Rafter escaped destruction and now provide an attractive façade to the many modern timber-working, paper-making, engineering and construction factories cited on the broad alluvial plain at the rivers' confluence. On the northern bank of the Oar, these old warehouses provide an attractive contrast with the many modern glass and steel offices and residential buildings situated among the old civic buildings (town hall, concert house, cathedral) that also survived the 1950 blaze. Since almost the entire city is pedestrianised (along with tram and cycle ways), it has been possible to space buildings in such a way as to minimise the risk of future possible fire damage while enhancing the cityscape with public squares and other small green spaces.

The ban on plastic throughout Dynamo, except for medical and electrical purposes, massively facilitates the re-cycling process since the glass/metal, organic, and paper/cardboard categories of waste are relatively easily submitted to reprocessing. Several experimental villages have recently been constructed in Spokane almost entirely based on re-cycled material, and powered by solar and water sources. The wooden hut style of chalet, with its traditional painted and carved decorations, has been maintained in Spokane (outside of Oarhouse), while the larger settlements and farmhouses continue to combine stone for the basements and cattle-sheds and wood for the habitable parts of the buildings. The region is also famous for its dairy products – in particular goats' cheeses and yoghurts – and its chocolate, the beans for which are imported from South America via St Sebastian and Gary. The most famous brand is Periwinkle, whose bright blue logo is also the badge of the province.

19: *Handlebar Mountains from the East* **by Alfred Sizzler**

Chapter 16

Urbanisation and Architecture

Like Britain and other countries of northern Europe, Dynamo Island combines Roman-originated classical and Gothic architectural traditions with, from the early twentieth century, a commitment to modernism in various guises. A national ethos in which human scale is seen as a priority means that few buildings in the country are truly monumental, architectural priorities being directed towards proportion, vernacular consistency and the use of local materials. There are no skyscrapers in any of the large cities, the height-limit for all buildings, except medieval churches or cathedrals with spires, being 50 metres. Dynamo's traditional celebration of the natural environment means that landscaping has always been an essential part of architectural design, with trees and greensward playing a vital role in building and planning projects. The national delight in verandas and other intermediary spaces between inside and outside and the high value placed on natural light has had a profound impact on architectural development. Roman domestic architecture, with its atriums and open central courtyards, colonnades and arcades has continued to exert its influence over two thousand years, to the extent that even in the modern period national or regional housing programmes often plan the construction of dwellings around shared courtyards or green spaces, in such a way as to promote sociability and neighbourliness while maintaining privacy. The plentiful supply of good stone and wood means that these materials are much used, though the qualities of concrete and other synthetic materials are also recognised and exploited. The importance of commerce, trade, sport, entertainment and other socially orientated human activities has meant that market places, theatres, sports grounds, parks and shopping streets have as far as possible been kept in the centre of towns and cities, intermingled with business and residential areas. In this way, the vitality of towns and cities has been maintained, with their centres being as animated at night as during the daytime.

20: View of Oarhouse, Spokane

Another distinctive feature of public or official buildings in Dynamo is the way that they are conceived in such a way as to convey to their viewers or users their meaning and purpose. As already noted, government buildings are as transparent and open to view as possible, with ministers and civil servants plainly to be seen going about their business. As in the Berlin Reichstag, the public may freely enter and observe from a special glazed viewing area the proceedings of the national assembly. The entrance to all ministries is marked by a panel indicating its business and purpose, with a list of the names of its main officials. The programme of debates at the Upper House or Senate, and those elected representatives participating in it, is relayed via a screen on the outside of the building while the principal articles enshrined in the national constitution are engraved in letters of gold on the façade of the National Assembly. Since much of the capital city of Veloxeter was modernised and reconfigured in the 1920s and 30s, the Art Deco style adopted in that period lent itself particularly well to elegant allegorical representation of the purpose of the building in question: so the National College of Art and Design, the National Library, the Athletics and Boxing Stadiums and the cinemas all incorporate bas-reliefs into their façades that depict the functions or activities associated with them. This forms part of the urban ethos of Dynamo whereby the city is conceived to be an arrangement that is both legible and beautiful, human in scale and purpose and yet inspiring in its elegance and transparency.

The absence of cars and lorries, or any heavy transport, massively facilitates the accessibility and freedom of the pedestrian or cyclist within urban areas: separate though often parallel tracks for pedestrians, cyclists, bicycle or small electric taxis, and trams means that the different tempos of travel can all be accommodated without any one type threatening another. The absence of diesel fumes means that both the air and the material fabric of the cities remains remarkably clean. The speed limit in all city centres for all conveyances, public or private, is 30km/h. Each track is asphalted in a different colour (grey paving for pedestrians, green for bikes, amber for electric vehicle, blue for trams) so that all users are aware of the route they should be following, thus radically reducing the incidence of accidents while enhancing the visual appeal of the streetscape. Road and cycle-track signage is geared at a level and scale appropriate to the user, with all signage coordinated in both colour and typeface in such a way as to conform to the principle of legibility and elegance that is central to the Dynamoan design ethos.

21: *Maurice Island* **by William Schooner**

Chapter 17

Maurice Island

Maurice Island (originally Moorish Island or Mauritius) was notorious in the seventeenth and eighteenth centuries as a base for Moorish and Dynamoan pirates who would launch attacks from southern Dynamo on British, French and Spanish shipping plying to and from the West Indies. The island, with its many hidden coves, plus the long estuary of the River Antinous stretching far into Pugilia leeward of the island, provided excellent cover. This banditry, often based also on capturing high-speed cutters used by the East India Company to deliver tea from China and India to London, eventually came to an end at the time of the Napoleonic Wars as the British Navy asserted its dominance in policing the Atlantic routes between Europe, America and the South Atlantic. The chief of the pirate bands, coincidentally named Maurice, was captured and hung from a gibbet in Quinnport Harbour in 1799. Since then, the Island's strategic position meant that it became an important naval centre for Dynamo, the home of the island's fleet, and an important docking and re-fuelling station. It was also the home of the merchant marine, whose college complemented that of the Dynamoan naval academy that was established in nearby Hadrianopolis later in the nineteenth century. The rivalry between the two colleges has traditionally been expressed in sporting competitions in rowing, sailing and, given Pugilia's pugilistic tradition, shipboard boxing. Today Quinnport is Dynamo's leading centre for the construction of yachts and other pleasure craft, while Hadrianopolis, capital of Pugilia, is the home of the country's main naval shipyards, established in the mid-nineteenth century to build iron-clad steamships on the model of those being developed in Britain.

An area of outstanding natural beauty, Maurice Island's tall chalk cliffs are the home of a remarkably varied maritime flora. The Thrift or Sea Pink, which is the island's symbol, along with the Sea Lavender and Burnet rose that cover the cliff-tops, swathe the island in a scented haze of pink and purple. The Island's position in the mid-Atlantic means that it is the breeding ground of many exotic as well as native seabirds, with Albatross, Booby, Tropic Birds, Bo's'un Birds and Tern making a regular appearance as well as the ubiquitous and round-season gulls, gannets, cormorants and dippers. The island forms part of the annual Tour of Dynamo cycling event, the steep coastal gradients making it a particularly spectacular stage in the competition. The hundreds of participants are ferried to the island from Hadrianopolis after the gruelling previous stage in the Ring Mountains in Pugilia and ferried back the following day, after which they pursue a more level course across Olympia to Odessa and then Spokane. Quinnport is the starting point of a number of famous yacht races: the annual Round-Mauritius Cup, the Dynamo Circuit, and the biennial Quinnport to Southampton and Quinnport to Nantucket races. Finally, the Antinous estuary and Mauritian coast provide excellent resorts for swimming and snorkelling and have as a result become popular holiday destinations.

Floating off to the east of Maurice Island is the smaller islet of Greer, home to an exclusively female community. Any woman seeking to escape male society is guaranteed a haven there, either permanently or temporarily, depending on individual circum-stances. Greer Island has its own school and college and is home to women of all ages. It is not populated exclusively by lesbians but by any women who for whatever reason prefer to live without male society. The community thus constitutes an interesting sociological experiment, not least in its commitment to ensure maximum protection of the natural environment. Indeed, the women of Greer are the guardians of one of Dynamo's rarest indigenous plants, *stachys muleris*, commonly known as Germaine-flower, a beautiful purple-flowered member of the *labiatae*, particularly valued for of its healing properties in relation to female ailments.

22: *Entry to Quinnport* **by Eric Ravisher**

Chapter 18

Education

The primary aim of education in Dynamo is to produce public-spirited and responsible citizens, with a wide knowledge of their own heritage and the natural environment, and a broad understanding of the wider world. Schooling begins at 5 years of age, with a shift at 12 years to secondary schooling. At 16 pupils have the choice either to move for a further two years to a technical or special skills college or to remain in school for two years to prepare for university entry. All education in Dynamo is nationally funded. There are no private schools. Sport and physical fitness are strongly promoted, with physical education forming part of every pupil's daily curriculum. The importance of a healthy diet and lifestyle is emphasised. Although there is liaison between teachers and parents, school is seen as being an independent institution in which pupils submit to a discipline and ethos that is not subject to interference from parents. All primary schools are co-educational but at secondary level students (in the larger cities at least) have the choice to opt for single-sex or co-educational institutions. Boarding is an option, in particular for students attending single-sex schools. All secondary school pupils wear a uniform. Sportswear at school is worn for sports only. All students at the age of 18, regardless of social or financial background, are obliged to complete one year of national service in the army, navy or airforce, or in a caring profession: medical or social welfare. In this way, students learn about the essential structures and values of Dynamo society and come into contact with a wide range of people and skills. Every student acquires a thorough knowledge of at least one foreign language, with a strong emphasis on European languages, including Latin. Philosophy and ethics are a compulsory part of the secondary-school curriculum.

In Dynamo, the university system is largely state-funded though many private firms also subvention specific research projects or establish professorships or centres. Universities are not run as commercial concerns but adhere to the ethos of universities in Britain and Europe before the 1980s when liberal economics began to undermine the academic freedom formerly taken for granted in third-level academic institutions. In other words, independent research as well as collaborative ventures (on a national as well as an international level) is highly valued and agendas from the world of industry and commerce are not imposed on third-level institutions. In Dynamo, undergraduate students do not pay university fees and are given a minimal maintenance grant if they choose to study at a university outside their home province. As in other countries in the European Union, a sabbatical year is either strongly encouraged or integral to every degree programme, and there are many exchange relationships with North American universities.

There are eight regional universities, one in each of the state capitals. The Hagel University in Odessa is the most prestigious owing to its cutting-edge research in physics and bioscience, but each of the eight leading universities has an international reputation in at least one of its key disciplines. The national observatory high in the Handlebar Mountains of Sparta, attached to Rugby University, is linked into a network of radio-telescopes in Europe and America, and Dynamoan scientists play an important role in the CERN project. Recycling, wind- and wave-power technology and hydroelectric engineering are key areas of Dynamoan technical expertise, as are train, tram and civic aeronautical research and development. The arts and humanities are as highly rated as the sciences in Dynamo: Anasi University has an internationally recognised film school, while Hubcaster is famous for its school of history and Veloxeter for its centre for creative writing. Dynamo's sports institutes in March, Boxcaster, Hadrianopolis, Odessa and Rugby attract students from all over the western world.

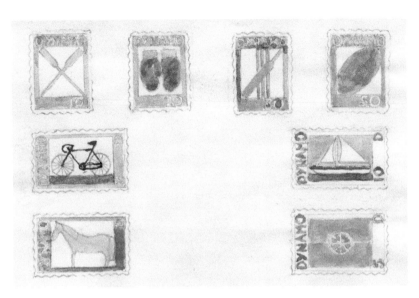

23: Dynamo Island stamps

Chapter 19

Pugilia and the Ring Mountains

In many ways Pugilia offers the most varied and dramatic scenery of Dynamo Island. The pasture and arable land of the northern part of the province rises dramatically in the south to the Ring Mountains, themselves carved into a spiral by the concentric circles of the River Antinous, which rises high up at the peak of Mount Eoin (3000 feet) and travels in a 200km loop to the broad estuary leading to the Atlantic. Mount Eoin rises like a clenched fist, one that local mythology ascribes to the local deity of that name, master of boxing, the sport in which, since Roman times, the province has most prided itself. The rich deciduous forests of the Ring Mountains still harbour wild boar and are famous for the truffles, much prized in Anasi restaurants, found in the beech-woods on the lower slopes. They are also home to the rare crimson-flowered boxglove that is the province's badge. Owing to their steep climbs and hairpin bends, the mountains are training grounds for cyclists, providing a testing range of biking challenges. The southern coast is particularly dramatic as the Ring Mountains' walls rise shear from the sea, followed by the main Anasi–Hadrianopolis railway that carves a tortuous route along a narrow coastal ledge, often having to plunge into tunnels blasted from solid rock before crossing the estuary of the River Antinous via a long suspension bridge.

Pugilia's two main cities, Boxcaster and Hadrianopolis, are of great historical importance. As its name suggests, Hadrianopolis was founded by the second-century Roman emperor who had sought shelter in the estuary of the river Hadrian, later named the Antinous, when blown off-course on a trip to Britannia. It was from the bridge-head of the camp established in this protected site that the Romans later began their campaign to invade the island as a whole, their first victory being achieved at Boxcaster, where a violent battle between them and the defending Celtic tribes (the *Velociae* and the *Pugiliae*) took place. The valour of the native Celtic tribes and their fighting skills, in unarmed as well as armed combat, was much appreciated by the Romans who, when they had pacified them, engaged their pugilistic skills as instructors in their army or sent them to Rome where they were much in demand as fighters in the Coliseum. The Celtic regional capital was renamed *Buxus castra*, where in today's Boxcaster, the association with boxing is reflected in the city's famous Luke Sheehan Boxing Academy. Hadrianopolis today is the most important port in the southern part of Dynamo, exporting timber, agricultural and manufactured goods. It is also an important shipbuilding centre and was, in the first half of the twentieth century, a major transatlantic passenger terminal.

24: *Mount Eoin, Pugilia* **by Henry Woodcock**

Chapter 20

Sport

Dynamo Island's strong martial tradition meant that from Roman times sport was encouraged among young men both as a preparation for military service but also as a beneficial activity in its own right. The Latin motto *Mens sana in corpore sano* became generally accepted, and physical culture recognised as important as social, moral and cultural development. The gymnasium thus became an integral part of education in Dynamo. The presence of violence in human life is recognised and sport encouraged as a means of giving a socially acceptable outlet to that violence. So, for example, boxing is a sport offered in all boys' schools and valued for the way it teaches respect for the other, physical courage, mental toughness and a spirit of fair play. Other Anglo-Saxon sports, in particular cricket and rugby, are similarly promoted nationally.

Another aspect of sport that is valued is the way it brings the human body into dynamic contact with the real or natural environment. Water sports – whether rowing, swimming, sailing or canoeing – all teach the sportsman and sportswoman much about the energy and resistance of natural phenomena such as wind, water, tide and current. Similarly, riding, hunting, shooting and fishing are practiced (under strict guidelines) so that humans enter into a vital and intelligent relationship with the natural world and, like indigenous tribes, learn to respect it even as they partly control it. There are no zoos in Dynamo and all farm animals and birds are permitted to range freely, the concept of 'factory farming' being rejected as an abomination. In this way, everyone is aware of natural processes and has a deeper understanding of the complexity of the ecological balance.

All Dynamoans, male and female, are encouraged to continue participating in sport throughout their lives. The strong social binding element of local and national teams and clubs is clearly recognised. Although, as in most of the rest of the world, some sports – in particular boxing, cricket, football and rugby – have become professionalised, the amateur participation in these and other sports is strongly encouraged, both by generous funding on a regional and a national level, and the provision of proper facilities in schools and regional towns as well as provincial capitals and large cities. With the turn-of-the-century revival of the Olympic spirit, centres of excellence were established with national academies of athletics (at Veloxeter's Halton Athletics Stadium), boxing (at Boxcaster), cricket (at March, home of the country's leading cricket team, the MCC), rugby (at Rugby), sailing at Quinnport on Maurice Island, and so on.

The country's leading national sport is cycling, with the national cycling academy established at Hubcaster. It is promoted not only as a sport but as a significant part of the Dynamoan ethos, one that promotes self-reliance, efficient expenditure of energy, health and fitness and a profound awareness of the environment in physical, meteorological and aesthetic terms. The annual Tour of Dynamo cycling competition, open to all ages and sexes, is for Dynamoans equivalent to every orthodox Moslem's ambition to make the pilgrimage to Mecca. It constitutes a celebration of the beauty of the natural world and the possibility of fruitful human interaction with it.

25: National sports-club badges

Chapter 21

A Multi-Cultural Society

Dynamo is a multiracial society. Though predominantly Anglo-Saxon/European, there are significant Jewish and to a lesser extent Arab communities present, in particular in the capital Veloxeter (population 1,750,000). Many Jews escaped to Dynamo from continental Europe during the Second World War whilst Arabs, in particular from North Africa, have settled in Veloxeter in some of the county's southern towns, in particular Anasi and Hadrianopolis. A significant number of Irish, fleeing the potato famines of the 1840s, settled in Dynamo, particularly in the northern regions, and contributed greatly to the development in the nineteenth century of the country's transport and industrial infrastructure. New Dublin, in the province of Sparta, is the centre of the Irish Diaspora and includes Guinness among its most notable manufactures.

Arab pirates set out on marauding expeditions from Maurice Island from the eighteenth century while Blacks of African extraction immigrated to Dynamo from the West Indies and the southern states of the USA in the 1960s. Since Dynamo's incursion into colonialism was short-lived – its eighteenth century skirmish with Great Britain over the ownership of the Caribbean island of Barbados was unsuccessful – there were in the post-colonial period of the later twentieth century no major influxes of African or West Indian blacks, though the country's general tolerance and fair immigration quotas made it an attractive destination. Dynamo was a popular destination in the late 1960s and early 1970s with hippies and others dissatisfied with US materialism and consumerism: in particular Arcadia was viewed as a kind of paradise for drop-outs who could buy up small holdings or limited tracts of land and live a more-or-less subsistence life-style. Limited growing of marijuana is still tolerated.

Dynamo has a significant community of travellers although, owing to the lack of cars, lorries and any sort of motor trade, their lifestyle has remained far closer to that of European gypsies in the pre-modern period. Once again, Arcadia, with its extensive woods, open pastureland and sparse settlements, provides the kind of wilderness within which certain travelling communities like to live. A limited level of poaching and produce misappropriation on the part of gypsies (they are still called this without any sense of a slur being attached to the term) is mostly tolerated by local country communities: there seems to be an unstated understanding between the two communities – the one static, the other mobile – that both have their rights which are tolerated provided neither side oversteps the mark. Dynamoan travellers still live in traditional horse-drawn caravans and make their living through tinkering, metal-work and wood carving (and also soft-drug pedalling). Their children are admitted to the state schools. As in Ireland, male travellers are celebrated for their prowess as boxers; their annual boxing jamboree held in the woods of Pugilia every midsummer is a key event in the sporting calendar.

Chapter 22

Challenges

The three main challenges facing the Republic of Dynamo in the contemporary world all relate in one way or another to the response of the country's inhabitants to the global capitalist world that seems likely to be the dominant ideological reality in the twenty-first century: how to maintain a zero-growth economy in an economic climate dominated by slow but nevertheless exponential global growth; how to satisfy the desires of a young generation in ways ultimately different and more authentic than those offered in a capitalist system constantly exposed to the blandishments of consumerist seduction; how to maintain a tolerant secular society, imbued with traditions developed over centuries, within a world of movement and cultural change.

The maintenance of a zero-growth economy is possible within a country in which government plays an active and constructive role in maintaining broad financial equality among its population and is flexible enough to respond to the inevitable shifts in economic developments with measures susceptible to maintaining full employment and a balanced productivity. The low dependence of Dynamo on energy imports means that it can continue, relatively unaffected by international market forces, to fuel a sophisticated technological and industrial society in which a prioritisation of sophisticated, ecologically favourable manufactures creates a growing export market while reinforcing the country's ideological stance. If unemployment ever exceeds the 5% mark, initiatives are immediately introduced to absorb inactive workers. This involves the development of a psychological attitude on the part of Dynamoans whereby all those employed, whether professionally or industrially, are prepared to adopt, if the necessity arises, a 'second' or fall-back occupation to which they can resort if made redundant, temporarily or permanently, from their first calling. The year of national service, carried out by all 18-year-olds, provides a training in a range of technical, social or military skills and is topped up every five years by a one-month refresher course, or a course in a new skill. Part of the ethos of the country is against the prevalent western trend towards ever greater specialisation: although specialisation is necessary for the development of science and technology, it need not be the prerogative of all members of the community who are as much encouraged to diversify as to specialise their skill base. The CVs of Dynamoan entrants to the employment market therefore would normally have at least two as opposed to one stated marketable skill.

Dynamo's young people, and indeed those of any age, are compensated for the unavailability of cars and motorbikes for individual use by the world's best public transport system, coordinating train, tram and bicycle systems, all of which are efficient, government-funded and affordable. The country's network of bike lanes and bicycle repair points is comprehensive and every train and tram running in the country has carriage for bikes. Individual creativity in music, cinema, sport and the arts is massively promoted in Dynamo, with many funding opportunities for creative people of any age. The country has a thriving pop music and independent cinema scene, the latter based in Anasi, which has become something of the Hollywood of Dynamo. Fashion is also an important industry in Dynamo, with a special focus on elegant cycle and riding wear. The town of Georgia is the centre of this, its fashion week in April being an important event in the international calendar. Veloxeter is the capital of the music industry though there are important pop festivals in Odessa, Upper March and Louisville.

The divide between the youth and the older members of the community is generally less wide than in other western countries. This is because Dynamoans generally keep very fit, continue to practice sports and other social activities well into their lives and try as far as possible to avoid an 'ageist' approach to any aspect of social activity. Tolerance of different sexual orientations has been institutionalised since the 1970s and the age of hetero- or homosexual consent (at 16) is lower than that of voting rights (18). Drugs are viewed in a way similar to alcohol or tobacco: they are heavily taxed but freely available, though hard drugs such as cocaine and heroin are very expensive and it is illegal to sell them to minors. The smoking of a joint is taken as the equivalent of drinking a pint of beer or a glass of whiskey. Smoking (of any substance) is however banned in all public buildings. The question of the use and abuse of drugs forms an integral part of Dynamoan secondary education, as do issues of civic and sexual responsibility. As a result, there is little drug-related crime in Dynamo, and, owing to effective government control of hard drugs, no drug mafia. People of all generations have a relaxed and tolerant view of the way fellow citizens choose to enjoy themselves, providing it does not harm or inconvenience others. Satisfaction-with-life indicators in Dynamo are therefore not measured in terms of wealth, prestige or televisual celebrity, but in happiness, personal fulfilment, creativity and social cohesion. Crime is looked upon as an aberration rather than a manifestation of evil, with punishment viewed as far as possible in terms of rehabilitation rather than incarceration. There is no capital punishment. With the exception of those in the armed forces, it is illegal to possess a firearm unless registered for use for shooting game, and to import any kind of gun or rifle from abroad.

The third major challenge facing Dynamo Island in the twenty-first century is that of how to maintain its distinctive traditions and ethos – secularity, harmony with and respect for the natural environment, regional pride and independence, social solidarity and yet recognition of individual difference – while increasingly exposed to the factitiousness, vulgarity, ostentation and triviality of western consumer and entertainment society. Television and radio, for example, are prohibited in all public places in Dynamo (except for special purposes), CCTV is strictly limited, and amplification of sound permitted only for licensed public events such as music festivals or sports matches. Silence, like clean air and privacy, is seen as a natural right, as far as possible in the towns as well as in the countryside. House alarms are banned and there are no police cars with wailing sirens: the police are unarmed and ride bicycles, though there are electric vehicles for police arrests and conveyance of the convicted. Only fire-engines and ambulances are permitted to use warning bells or sirens.

There are four national TV channels, two of which are government run, the other two being open to independent national franchises. None of them is commercial and there is therefore no advertising, except for national or local cultural, sporting or other events. This does not prevent every individual in the country from having free access to the internet and to foreign television channels. Advertising is of course allowed in newspapers and on the internet but, outside the cities, billboards are banned. Tram stops and railway platforms are however richly endowed with advertising space, so Dynamoan graphic design thrives as it produces posters advertising travel, holiday destinations and regional specialities. Graphic design in general – whether it be in relation to postage stamps, government information, books as well as posters – is highly rated in Dynamo which, like the Netherlands in the twentieth century, recognises that the means and media of representation are as important as the message relayed and potentially as exemplary of the culture in question as any other aspect of it.

About the Author

David Scott holds a personal chair in French (Textual & Visual Studies) at Trinity College Dublin. He has written widely on literature, painting and textual/visual studies, and organized a number of exhibitions on art and design. Using semiology as a theoretical framework, he has published books on aesthetics, poetics and graphic design. A middle-weight amateur boxer, he has also published two books on boxing, while his love of travel, real or imaginary, is reflected in his study entitled *Semiologies of Travel* (2004), as well as in *Dynamo Island*. He is currently working on a volume of short stories entitled *Cut up on Copacabana*. His website is at http://dynamodave.com.

Previous publications

Pictorialist Poetics
(Cambridge University Press, 1988; paperback 2009)

Paul Delvaux: surrealizing the nude
(Reaktion Books,1992)

European Stamp Design: a semiotic approach
(Academy Editions, 1995)

Semiologies of Travel: from Gautier to Baudrillard
(Cambridge University Press, 2004)

The Art and Aesthetics of Boxing
(The University of Nebraska Press, 2009)

Poetics of the Poster: the rhetoric of image/text
(Liverpool University Press, 2010)

Cultures of Boxing
(Oxford: Peter Lang, 2015)

Contemporary culture has eliminated both the concept of the
public and the figure of the intellectual. Former public spaces –
both physical and cultural – are now either derelict or colonized
by advertising. A cretinous anti-intellectualism presides,
cheerled by expensively educated hacks in the pay of
multinational corporations who reassure their bored readers
that there is no need to rouse themselves from their interpassive
stupor. The informal censorship internalized and propagated by
the cultural workers of late capitalism generates a banal
conformity that the propaganda chiefs of Stalinism could only
ever have dreamt of imposing. Zer0 Books knows that another
kind of discourse – intellectual without being academic, popular
without being populist – is not only possible: it is already
flourishing, in the regions beyond the striplit malls of so-called
mass media and the neurotically bureaucratic halls of the
academy. Zer0 is committed to the idea of publishing as a
making public of the intellectual. It is convinced that in
the unthinking, blandly consensual culture in which we live,
critical and engaged theoretical reflection is more important
than ever before.